Black Francis McHugh

Proinsias Dubh Mac Aodha

An Irish Highway Man of the 18th Century

29th January 2010

By Joe O'Loughlin Joe O'Loughlin

Black Francis McHugh
Proinsias Dubh Mac Aodha
An Irish Highway Man of the 18th Century

Design & Layout: Diamond SignPrinting Ltd.
Illustrations: Jane O'Loughlin

PREFACE

Having had the opportunity to read the manuscript of this short story by my friend Joe O'Loughlin I found it to be enjoyable and entertaining. If I were to find a fault with it, I think that the plot is good enough to have made a considerably longer and more detailed story. But then this is his style and any major change might detract from it.

I have in the course of my own research travelled all around the district where Proinsias Dubh plied his trade including a visit to Carn graveyard where he is reputed to have been buried. Therefore I am quite familiar with the area.

Eileen Hewson, F.R.G.S.
Kabristan Archives,
Old Irish and Indian graveyards.

PROLOGUE

The fourteen year old McHugh twins Edward and Katie were on their usual summer holiday visit in 1950 to their Grandma Jane McHugh who lived in the small town of Lithgow which was about 50 miles west of their home on the outskirts of Sydney. Their parents had a general store in Sydney; the twins had an elder brother and a sister who remained at home to help with the family business. Their father – Francis who was born in 1894 had served with the Australian army in Europe from 1916 until 1918 during the First World War. He also served in an administrative capacity in England during the Second World War. He was in England from 1942 until 1945. Francis was married in 1926 and the twins who are the youngest were born in 1936, naturally they missed their father a lot when he was away from the home. The house Grandma Jane lived in was very old, this was the house that the first McHugh to come to Australia from Ireland many years ago, had built. Since then it had been renovated and extended on several occasions. A young Jane Ward had married Edward McHugh in 1890 and lived here ever since. After her husband died in 1840 Jane rented the large farm to neighbouring farmers as none of her family had an interest in operating the land. Jane was very alert for her age – 84 years and she loved to have the twins stay with her. Several Aboriginal families had their own homes on the farm. Grandma told the twins how when the first McHugh founded the farm over 150 years ago he employed a number of the native people to work for him. He treated them very well and so gained their respect. He built houses for them to live in and granted ownership to the families. Their descendants still lived in the homes and the twins would play with their youngsters.

In the country there was a group called the Australian Returned Service Men's Association. This body raised funds for the men who had served in both World Wars and also for the families of those who died during the wars or since then. The local branch was organising a car boot sale to raise funds. Grandma Jane asked the twins to go up to her attic and see if they could find some useful items to donate towards the sale. Of course the children were only too delighted to get into 'Grandma's Attic'. They climbed up the stone steps which were built against the outer back wall unlocked the padlock on the door with its key and entered that part of the attic that was over the new section of the building. Grandma warned them to be very careful and gave them two torches to use. They had a wonderful time uncovering items that had not been used for many years. There were old toys belonging to the children, pieces of old but good furniture and some landscape paintings. Having removed everything down into the yard for inspection by Grandma they then proceeded to clean and leave the items in a good condition. The children soon had the items in a presentable condition for collection. Grandma had many stories to tell about the things and the family members who had used them. The twins had observed a door in a partition separating the new part of the attic from the old part which was over the original house. They tried the keys on the bunch they had been given to open the lock. One was the right fit but would not turn, so they got some oil which they poured into the lock, after some time they got the key to turn and opened the door. As there were no lights or windows in the apartment they returned into the house to ask Grandma's permission to search the attic. She had warned them they might see nothing of any value and were about to leave when they spotted a large object almost hidden out of sight away in a corner under the roof. Going over to it they removed several old blankets covering the object and there they found an old travel trunk. By the light of the torches they could make out some lettering in the lid.

Taking a handle it each end of the trunk Edward and Katie dragged it across the floor and through the door into the new part of the Attic where there was much more light. The children got a damp sponge and cleaned the outside of the trunk. On the lid two names that had been painted there became clear, they were Francis and Molly McHugh passengers on the good ship 'MINERVA' sailing from Dublin, Ireland to Sydney, Australia. 1783. The hasps of the lid were not locked, so with the aid of a screwdriver they got the lid prised open. It was obvious that this trunk had been constructed by a skilled craftsman; the dove tailed joints were perfectly made. A tray was set on wooden runners just beneath the lid, the tray was empty. On lifting it out the children found several bundles of old letters, which had come from Ireland many years ago. They would read them later. A large paper wrapped parcel was next to claim their attention, opening it they found a very old home spun dress, which was in remarkable good condition apart from several buttons that were missing, only two were left on the garment, which also had a strong double leather belt. Taking the wet sponge Edward decided to clean the inside of the trunk, the natural grain of the oak wood returned to its original colour.

Edward felt a movement on a broad long board that made part of the floor of the trunk. On closer examination he saw that it had not been nailed or screwed in position. There was a small knot hole in the timber; with the aid of the screwdriver Edward gently lifted the board. There in the secret compartment was another package wrapped in fine leather and tied with hemp. Lifting out the package Edward replaced the tray in the trunk and closing down the lid the young people unwrapped the parcel and there found a leather bound journal. It soon became obvious that this was a history of the McHugh family going back to the second half of the eighteenth century in Ireland. The young people started to read and soon were engrossed by the story that unfolded before their eyes. This what they found . . . .

PRIONSIAS DUBH MAC AODHA

(Black Francis McHugh)

CHAPTER 1

There is a point in the Irish province of Ulster where the three counties of Donegal, Fermanagh and Tyrone meet. At this place a man could have a foot in each of two counties and his walking stick resting in the third one. Only in Ireland could such a situation arise. It was in this general district that one famous Ulsterman was born and reared in the second half of the eighteenth century. To the poor people who suffered so much from ruthless landlords and who benefited from the exploits of Highway Man - Proinsias Dubh Mac Aodha, he came a close second in the folklore to St. Patrick himself who had established Christianity in this part of the country. To the landed gentry he was the cause of much concern especially when he relieved them of their ill-gotten goods and cash accumulated from the unjust rents collected from the poor tenants. To these people he was known by the English version of his name – Black Francis McHugh, highway man, outlaw and rebel, a man with a price on his head. It was on an island of nearby Lough Derg that St. Patrick had founded the world famous place of penance that for centuries has been visited by pilgrims from all over Europe.

The entry of Francis McHugh into this world did not happen in the traditional Irish way, he was not alone in this respect as the birth of many Irish children was the result of landed gentry who took advantage of innocent young Irish girls who were forced by circumstances to take up employment in the big houses and often in the castles of the planter stock who had confiscated the lands and property of the native Irish. Francis's mother, Moyia was the third and youngest child of John and Kate McHugh, who having been evicted from their farm near Lettercran on the Donegal/Tyrone border were forced to live in a cabin in the town land of Curraghmore in County Fermanagh on the shores of Lough Erne. They had two sons – James and young John, known as Jack. John McHugh was a good worker and had learned the trade of blacksmithing while serving in the English army. From the army he had a small pension that enabled him to feed his family and pay the exorbitant rent to the landlord on the small holding. Kate was an industrious lady and an expert needle worker, she was often called upon to nurse and treat sick people, her knowledge of the old Irish cures that had been handed down in her family from generation to generation was exceptional. She kept a stock of native herbs and so could treat many complaints. Between them they eked out a living. The soil on their holding in Curraghmore was of poor quality, one small section was just about good enough to grow a crop of potatoes and some vegetables. The rest of it was almost a swamp; several hundred years ago it had been a lake that at one time drained away.

Many centuries back in the history of Ireland when Curraghmore was mostly a lake there had been a dwelling in the centre of the water. It had been built on an artificial island.

This type of dwelling was called a crannog. To reach it from the shore there was a secret underwater causeway that was known only to the people who lived on the crannog. For safety in times of danger the families could take refuge here and also bring their livestock out from the shore. By the time John and Kate came to live in Curraghmore practically all traces of the crannog had disappeared. It was from the local folklore handed down by the storytellers from one generation to another that John learned of the existence of the ancient dwelling place. Never having had a formal education John had learned to read and write while in the army, he was a highly intelligent man. He decided to investigate the centre of the swamp and by probing with a long pole he located the hidden step stones that had been part of the secret causeway. It took him a long time, something that he had in abundance. Often he would miss the pathway and sink into the quagmire. He learned from this experience to place a strong pole in a secure place and attach a rope to it. Eventually he located the foundations of the original crannog and placed his own secret markings to guide him along the causeway.

Because of his skill as a blacksmith and his expertise with horses John was often called upon by the local gentry to exercise his trade. A cautious and reserved person by nature, he took care not to become too friendly with either the gentry or their agents. Very often the agents were more of a danger to the local inhabitants than the landed people. They were constantly on the lookout for any signs of unrest in the population, for there was always the threat of an uprising or of a rebellion against the ruthless ruling class. Anything of this nature was immediately reported to the authorities by men for a meagre reward. Those who were considered guilty of an offence were dealt with in the most ruthless fashion. The informer who gave information to the authorities was ostracised not only by neighbours but also by immediate family members. For centuries the informer was the scourge of the Irish nation.

The landlord for the area, Sir Albert Melgard, lived about 70 miles away in Castle Leslough, his agent Benjamin Badham lived in Ardnamona House. From here he managed the affairs of the estate for Sir Albert, he hired the employees, collected the rent; decided which tenant should remain in their home and which should be evicted. In the big house lived Benjamin's wife, Heather, daughter, Edith and son Jeffery. The domestic staff members were under the control of Miss Jenkins the housekeeper. The gardens, stables, byres, workshop and other outhouses were supervised by the land steward, Derek Hogge. A former soldier, he ruled the workforce in military fashion.

When Moyia was 17 years old she was sent into service with her cousin Sarah Anne Corrigan to work in Ardnamona House. Moyia was a very pretty young woman with a well developed figure. She was dark haired with attractive green eyes and a lovely smile. The house was big, dark and dreary, rather frightening for young girls who had been brought up in a small cabin. Miss Jenkins took them in charge, showed them their living quarters, which were in a small building to the rear of the family dwelling. They were given strict instructions regarding their duties and their conduct, how to behave in the presence of the master, mistress and family members. Wages if any would be small and only payable once a year if their work was satisfactory. Moyia and Sarah were introduced to other members of staff and were pleased to find that they already knew two of them, Ellen McCaffrey and Mary Sweeney. A brother of Mary's, Edward Sweeney worked in the stables with the horses, a very pleasant young man about two years older than Moyia, he was nice to her and often when the occasion arose they talked together. The girls if they were lucky and of good conduct might be permitted to visit their homes every two months. Occasionally there would be something to brighten the life of Moyia. Her father John and her brother Jack would arrive at the stables to shoe horses and to repair the carriage, farm machinery and other vehicles. It was not easy to escape from the watchful eyes of Miss Jenkins, but the other girls would make some excuse to have the housekeeper attend to duties in a part of the house well away from the stables and the farmyard, thus giving Moyia the chance to spend some time with her father and brother.

The work of the domestic staff was hard cleaning, polishing, dusting, window cleaning and a host of other duties, bed linen had to be changed regularly, laundered and ironed. The hours were long. The girls started early in the morning at 6am preparing and serving the family breakfast including doing the dishes. In the evening everything had to be cleared up after the dinner, only then were the members of staff permitted to retire to their sleeping quarters. If there were guests staying or a party on some special occasion there was extra work to be done.

CHAPTER 2

One day when Moyia had been working in the house for about six months she and Ellen McCaffrey were sent to the upper floor to change bed linens and clean the rooms. When this work had to be done the chambermaids always worked in pairs, one of the more experienced girls would accompany the new members of staff. When work on some of the rooms had been completed Ellen had to go the linen room for more sheets and pillow cases. This room was at the other end of the house. As Moyia continued with her duties she heard a sound behind her, turning around she was surprised to see Mr. Jeffery standing behind her. He had a most evil and dangerous look on his face. He grabbed Moyia and tore her clothes off her and proceeded to assault her in a most vicious manner. Then he raped the young girl who was screaming for help. Moyia had no idea of what was happening to her, being an innocent virgin she had no sexual experience whatsoever. She only knew that something terrible was being done to her. When Jeffery had exhausted himself with this wild attack, he collapsed beside the terrified girl. She found his head beside hers, from some where she found the strength to try and escape. His ear was just beside her mouth, some thing inspired her to bite the lower part of his ear with her sharp teeth. Jeffery was enraged by this attack on him and with the shock of the pain he wrenched his head away, in doing so the lower part of his ear was cut away. Moyia with some super human strength managed to break away from his clutches, the blood was streaming from the open wound. The assailant was roaring in rage and in a state of shock. Moyia gathered her disarranged clothes around her and ran from the room in terror. As she ran along the corridor he was gaining on her, at the top of the stair way was a large flower vase standing on a table. Moyia flung this into the path of her attacker and he fell headlong over it, tumbled down the stairs with the blood streaming from his wound. He then collapsed unconscious at the bottom of the steps.

Moyia in her terrified state had only one thing on her mind and that was to get away from this place where she had been so ruthlessly vilified. There was only one place where she wanted to be and that was with her mother and her family in her own home. She did not even think of going to her quarters for her belongings. Nobody had heard the commotion, which really had only lasted for a short time. Benjamin Badham, along with his wife and daughter where away travelling, Miss Jenkins had retired to her quarters for her afternoon nap. Obviously Jeffery had kept the girls under observation and taking his chance had carried out the vicious attack on the young girl. Moyia rearranged her clothes as best as possible and ran as quickly as she could away from the big house. After running for several miles she was so exhausted that she collapsed on the road side. As chance would have it, Edward Sweeney was returning to the house in a pony and trap having been sent to another part of the estate to carry out some duties. He immediately stopped and even in her distressed state he recognised his friend Moyia. Her clothes were torn and covered in blood; Edward feared that she was seriously injured.

He comforted her and placed her in the trap with the intention of bringing her back to the big house. He asked her what had happened and she told him how she had been attacked and assaulted by the son of the owner of the house. She was terrified at the idea of going back there and said the only place she wanted to be was at home with her family. Edward knew full well the kind of scoundrel that Jeffery Badham was. He also knew that this was not the first time that he had taken advantage of an innocent young girl. He turned around the trap and set off for Curraghmore with his young friend. Edward knew that the other Badham family members were away from the house and that he had plenty of time to get Moyia to her family. As she was trembling with shock and fear Edward took off his coat and wrapped it around the young girl. When they reached the McHugh cabin Edward brought her into the house and placed her in the care of her mother. He briefly explained to her father what had happened and said that he would have to return to the big house before the owners came back. He promised to come back as soon as possible to see Moyia.

Her mother Kate did every thing possible to comfort her daughter while John stood by; naturally he was outraged by what had happened. Kate removed the soiled uniform from Moyia, washed her carefully and dressed her in clean clothing. During this Kate discovered the large piece of severed ear and asked her daughter what it was. On being told, she decided that it should be preserved with the possibility of it being used as evidence again Jeffery Badham. She found a small jar and filled it with poteen, (the home brewed Irish spirit) this she put in a safe place. With Moyia comforted and put to her bed, Kate and John discussed the terrible experience that their daughter had come through. They were determined to support Moyia no matter what the consequences of the brutal attack might be. They were aware of the possibility that their daughter might find herself with child. They also knew that it would be pointless for a poor family to take any action against the assailant, for it would be his peers who would judge any case and they would not condemn one of their own.

Meanwhile back in the house there was pandemonium, the Master and Mistress had returned home to find the place in uproar. Their son was covered in blood, a portion of his ear missing and as a result of his fall down the stairs he had broken a leg. Miss Jenkins had been trying to bring some kind of order to the situation. Mr. Benjamin followed the trail of blood to the bedroom where the assault had taken place; there was enough evidence to show him that some person had been seriously abused. It was then discovered that one of the young domestic staff was missing, Moyia McHugh was nowhere to be found. An extensive search of the property found no trace of her. A doctor had been summoned to attend the injured Jeffery; his outraged father questioned him as to how he received such serious injuries. He was not so much annoyed that an innocent young girl had been defiled by his son, but rather that he had been caught in the act. Edward Sweeney had returned to the house in the midst of all this and observed from a discreet distance all that was going on. It was obvious to him that the family had no consideration or thought to the victim, their only concern was for their disgraced son.

Edward would bide his time and let his sister Mary and her friend Ellen know where Moyia now was.

It was the following day before Edward got an opportunity to tell Ellen and Mary that Moyia was now safe at home with her parents in their cabin in Curraghmore. The girls planned that they would both visit their friend on their day off. Considering what had happened, Miss Jenkins was agreeable to let them both have a day off together. Back in the cabin Moyia's parents did every thing possible to comfort her and assured her that never again would she have to return to Ardnamona. Edward called to see her at any available opportunity for he was very fond of his young friend. As the weeks passed by the worst fears of Kate McHugh were confirmed and Moyia was found to be with child. This made the family more determined than ever to support their daughter in this time of great need. They knew that it would be futile to make any approach to the Badham family for any assistance. Kate and John were highly intelligent people. They firmly believed in the old Irish saying that the Lord never closed one door but that he would some time open another one. If they were patient they could make the villainous Jeffery Badham pay for his crime against the young girl. The months passed by and it became near the time for the birth of the baby. Ellen, Mary and Edward were regular visitors to the cabin. The young people brought all the latest news from the big house and the goings on of the family. John himself occasionally went to the stables there, to shoe horses and repair traps, carriages and carts. This did not bring him into direct contact with the family, nevertheless being very observant and listening to the staff he had a good knowledge of what was going on. He also knew that Sir Albert Melgard made regular visits to this part of his estate to check up on how it was being managed. A sizeable part of his income came from the rents of the tenants and Benjamin was responsible for collecting the money.

As the time drew near for the birth of the baby a family friend who was what was known locally as the Handy Woman (the fore runner of the modern mid-wife) came to the cabin to give her expert assistance. Early in the morning of 4th October 1760 a fine healthy boy was born; he was in appearance a real McHugh and bore no resemblance to his natural father. He had a fine head of very black hair and as he was born on the feast day of St. Francis he was given that name. So from his earliest days he was known by the Gaelic form of his name as Prionsias Dubh Mac Aodha. With the care and attention of a loving mother and her family the infant thrived and was a great favourite with everyone, especially with Edward Sweeney who looked upon the child as his own son.

Back in the big house Benjamin Badham was becoming senile in his advancing years. His wife Heather, who had social ambitions above her station in life was anxious to groom her wayward son to succeed his father as the agent for Sir Albert Melgard on the estate. For this to become feasible it was essential that Jeffery should settle down in life and acquire a wife of some standing in the community. A rather difficult situation, as his reputation was quite well known in upper class circles. Through her friends, Heather found out about a Miss Elisabeth Ackerman, an eligible lady who would be socially acceptable in their class. Elisabeth had had a number of suitors but so far she had rejected them even though she would soon be past her prime and in danger of being left on the shelf. Not an ideal situation for a lady of her standing. The usual discreet enquiries were made which eventually led to Elisabeth being introduced to Jeffery and in due course a betrothal was arranged. Not being blessed with good looks the all important details of the dowry that Elisabeth would bring with her to compensate for this, details were settled. This was very important as the financial affairs of the Bedham family were not in a healthy state. During the party season many events were attended by the couple and their families got to know each other, both hoping that the match would lead to the expected wedding, which it did.

It was decided for several reasons that the wedding should take place in the Church near to the Badham residence. The Dean of the diocese was the rector of the parish and he would perform the ceremony, which promised to be the most important social event of the year in the district. Plans were made for a most elaborate reception for the many guests who were to be invited. A special room was set aside for the display of the large number of valuable presents given to the couple. On a lovely May morning everything was in place, outside the church colourful bunting decorated the avenue leading to the building. Inside there was a beautiful display of flowers. The fashionable dresses and elegant hats worn by the ladies were admired by the onlookers who had gathered for the occasion. The courtyard was filled with coaches and other fine vehicles. The coachmen were being entertained in a suitable Irish manner by the stable staff. Shortly after the time appointed for the ceremony to commence the bride and her entourage arrived and walked up the isle to the accompaniment of suitable organ music. Led by the verger, the Dean in full clerical robes emerged from the vestry to greet the bride and groom.

For some time past in the McHugh cabin the family had been made aware of the forthcoming marriage of Jeffery and Elisabeth. Edward had by his discreet powers of observation become acquainted with the full plans for the big day. Moyia and her family felt that the event could not be allowed to pass without some form of attention being drawn to the terrible wrong that Jeffery had done to Moyia. Little baby Francis was developing into a lovely pleasant child with favourable qualities that endeared him to all. While the McHugh family had been suppressed for generations by cruel landlords their natural intelligence and brilliant brains could never be suppressed. A plan was drawn up to expose the cruel and oppressive Jeffery for the villain that he really was.

In the church the Dean had commenced with the wedding ceremony and had reached the stage where he said,
'If anyone here present can show cause why Jeffery and Elisabeth should not be joined in Holy Matrimony will they now speak or for ever hold their peace?'
As the Dean paused for a moment in silence a young woman holding a child emerged from the vestry door unto the sanctuary. She wore a veil over head, held a child on one

arm and in her hand she carried a small glass jar. The full congregation was left speechless by this intrusion. The young woman said, "Nearly two years ago I was violently attacked and raped by that man, pointing to Jeffery Badham, while employed in his home. I was left with this child. In trying to defend myself I bit off the half of his left ear. It is preserved in this jar and I give it now, to you the bride, so that you may have a whole man". The jar was placed on the silver salver along with the rings, which were ready to be blessed. All was over in seconds and before the congregation had realised what had happened the young woman disappeared into the vestry. Once there she locked the door with its big key, from the outside she also locked the entrance door and flung the key into the trees.

Moyia ran a short distance up the avenue to where Edward was waiting out of sight in a pony and trap, there were no witnesses to see them, and soon Moyia was once again safe in the McHugh cabin. Back in the church there was pandemonium, Elisabeth had fainted and efforts were made to bring her around. Jeffery was completely stunned by this intrusion, one of his comrades pulled back the long hair to see for himself the damage done to his ear. When order was eventually restored there was a serious consultation amongst the families. The immediate families could not gain access to the vestry, the verger was sent to his home to get a spare key for the outside door. Everything had to be sorted out in full view of the guests; Elisabeth being a very strong willed person knew that as bad as the situation was she must go ahead with the wedding ceremony. Her dowry had already been given over; there would never again be a chance now to find another man to marry her. What nobody else knew was that she was in the early stages of being with child. So in spite of the humiliation she had suffered she insisted that the ceremony go ahead.

No matter how embarrassing the situation had become the guests had no alternative only to go along with the ceremony. Nobody had any idea who the young woman had been; for Jeffery there was no argument or excuse that he could give. The preserved portion of his ear was conclusive evidence against him. It was to be several days before an account of the event came through to the McHugh cabin. At last an opportunity had presented itself to make Jeffery Badham pay for his crime, he had no idea what the future had in store for him. For it was at his own peril that he should have interfered with a member of the McHugh clan.

CHAPTER 3

After the marriage life in the Ardnamona returned to a routine, which it can be said was just not quite normal. Old Benjamin's health deteriorated and he was no longer able to carry out his duties as agent for Sir Albert Melgard, his son Jeffery was appointed to replace him. Within a few months Benjamin had passed away. His wife Heather had moved out of the big house to reside in a vacant house a short distance away. Their daughter Edith had gone to live with her aunt in England. Elisabeth was in full control in the house and following her humiliating experience at her wedding she dominated the life of her husband. It cannot be said that the newlyweds settled down to a blissful and happy married life. Jeffery had been exposed for the person that he really was, he had acquired a bride of standing in the area and also a substantial dowry that went some way to relieving the financial difficulties of his family. Elisabeth had become a respected member of society as well and at last had found a husband. She did not permit her husband to enjoy the normal relationship that would be part of married life, so she moved into a separate room in their home

As the time came near for the birth of the expected child, Elisabeth moved to live with an aunt in the county town. This would mean that the early arrival of an off spring would not be known by local people. In due course a healthy baby girl – Jennifer - was born, Elisabeth was determined that this would be the only child of the marriage. There would never be a legitimate male heir to the Big House. Jeffery proceeded to carry out the duties of agent for Sir Albert, he had a cunning brain and soon he had devised a method to ensure that he had a private income from the estate. He was careful not to over do his illegal activities. All the records were kept in his office and nobody had access to this room. He was responsible for the collection of the rents from the tenants of the estate. He falsified the ledgers to show that here were a lesser number of tenants than there really were. He increased rents without informing Sir Albert; he recorded the supposed deaths of animals that he had sold. If a cow had twin calves only one was entered it the books. If twelve bags of grain were received from the mill he only entered ten. Wages were paid to non existing employees and many expenses were falsely recorded. Jeffery was astute enough to have the estate show a reasonable profit, so Sir Albert did not suspect anything unusual. He used the ill gotten gains to finance a life style that was considerably above his means.

Edward Sweeney still worked on the estate; principally he was responsible for the horses and the upkeep of the stables and the various wheeled vehicles and machinery belonging to the big house. Edward was a highly intelligent young man and with his good powers of observation he had a fair idea of what was going on. Occasionally Edward would be called by Jeffery into the office to receive instructions on various matters, he had been promoted to take over many of the duties of the land steward, Derek Hogge who was now of advanced years and not as capable as he had been in the past of supervising the work to be done. When Elisabeth took over the management of the house she dismissed Miss Jenkins's, whose ideas of managing a big house and its staff were rather outdated. Sarah Corrigan and Edward's sister Mary had found work elsewhere so only Ellen McCaffrey of the original group of girls still remained on the domestic staff. In Jeffery's office there was a large cabinet that was always kept locked and never opened in the presence of Edward. One day quite by chance he observed from a distance, when Jeffery was not aware that he was nearby, where the key to the cabinet was kept. Jeffery had cut a groove into the top edge of the big door into his office and it was there that he kept the key in its secret hiding place. All this Edward kept to himself, there might come a day when such information could prove to be extremely valuable.

One day when Jeffery was away, Edward unobserved went into the office and taking the key from its hiding place he locked the door and opened the secure cabinet. In it were two sets of books, one were the official account books for inspection by Sir Albert, the other set recorded the details of the embezzlement activities of his employee. There was also a drawer containing a considerable amount of gold and silver coins the result of the fraud carried out by Jeffery. Very carefully Edward left everything as he had found it, returned the key to it place on the top of the door. He was not tempted to take any of the contraband gold, the knowledge he had gained was something he could put to a good use at some future time. He carried out his normal duties in a way that did not cause his employer to doubt in any way the trust that he had placed in him.

Back in Curraghmore young Francis was developing into a fine strong boy. Edward was a regular visitor to the McHugh homestead for he had fallen in love with Moyia and treated Francis like a son. He had on a few occasions asked Moyia to marry him, she said that she would give his proposal serious consideration, but she did not want to burden Edward with another man's child. Within a short time a nearby cabin became vacant as the family who lived in it had decided to emigrate to America. Edward approached Jeffery and was granted the tenancy of the cabin, which although needing some repairs was in reasonable condition. Together with Moyia's father, John, he carried out all the necessary work and soon he had a comfortable home. Moyia had talked over the situation with her parents and when next Edward asked her to marry him she consented. At that time due to the penal laws in Ireland, there was no priest residing in the area. Occasionally a travelling friar would come to celebrate Mass and administer the sacraments in secret places. Through his friends Edward learned of a priest who was performing his duties some distance away. He borrowed a pony and trap and Moyia, himself and baby Francis travelled to the safe house where the priest was staying. The young couple were married and Francis was baptised and given the name Francis McHugh Sweeney. Now they were a complete family and set up their home in the rented cabin.

CHAPTER 4

As John McHugh got older he decided to pass on the secret of the passage to Edward, "Saying some day you will find the hidden island very useful. You in turn can pass on the details to young Francis". John's own son Jack, had plans made to emigrate to Australia where some members of the McHugh family already lived.

In due course young Jack made his way to Australia, a willing and skilful worker he had no problem finding work. Life was not that easy for many Irish people had been transported to the country and were treated as criminals. James McHugh the other son took over the farming duties from his father and occasionally when required would assist with work in the big house. After two years of married life Moyia and Edward were blessed with another child – a girl – who was called Mary Sarah after Edward's sister and Moyia's cousin and great friend. They were now a complete family and young Francis was most proud of his little sister. Life was not easy in those times for a growing family, John McHugh took a great interest in his grandson, he taught him how to read and write; some thing that very few young people had the opportunity to learn. While he was still able to do so he took young Francis around the area, instructed him on wildlife and how much could be learned from the animals and birds. He also showed him how to reach the crannog by the hidden causeway and warned him never to show it to anyone outside their own family.

John told him all about his life in the army and what the foreign lands were like. He passed on the great knowledge he had of the history of Ireland and of how the people had suffered under unjust rulers. He told Francis that some day all this would change, but it would take many years for this to come to pass. "The knowledge I am passing on to you will someday be very useful and may even save your life." Not alone did Francis learn much from his grandfather that would prove to be useful in the future, his Grandmother taught him many things about the old days and the old ways of life, she told him the stories that had been handed down in her family for generations. Kate was a fluent speaker in the Gaelic language, this she passed on to her grandson, she knew that to understand and appreciate the history of Ireland the only way to do so was through the native language. Many other young folk in the area had a good working knowledge of the Gaelic. The years went by and Francis grew up to be a fine strong and knowledgeable youth. When he was old enough to understand such matters his parents told him the story of his coming into this world. While Edward was still working at the big house he seldom brought Francis near the place. There were changes in the McHugh family when in 1775 John passed away, followed within the year by the death of Kate. Both were buried in the old Carn graveyard just across the county boundary in Donegal.

Living conditions were, for most families in the area spartan; they lived in poor houses, mostly mud cabins with at the most a sleeping room along with the kitchen. The roof was of thatch, the windows and doorway very small. A small fire used turf and wood to heat the room and cook the meals. The only local employment was with the often ruthless landlord and was a form of slave labour, usually poorly paid. The families were only tenants of the landlord who owned all the property and demanded an annual rent for it. Non payment meant eviction and the family left homeless. The principal food was the humble potato and a few other vegetables. Some families managed to rear a pig, which when ready was killed and the pork and other ingredients would be shared with neighbours who were in great need. The head of the house often assisted by his sons would supplement the food supply by poaching rabbits and fish. These were of course the property of the landlord and to be caught with them meant instant eviction and often imprisonment.

This was the situation in Ireland when young Prionsias Dubh was growing up in Curraghmore. With the skills passed on to him by his grandfather – John; he became an expert in hunting and fishing. He did his poaching over a wide area, seldom going twice to the same place; this lessened the chance of him being caught by the bailiffs. He shared his catches with many of his less well off neighbours. With the death of John; closely followed by that of Kate, the family lost the small but valuable income from the army pension. Generally in the area living conditions became worse, there was no work for the ordinary person, food was hard to get and only for the potato and some vegetables the people would have starved.

From the age of 15 onwards Francis and some friends of his age would at night go poaching for fish and eels, they also hunted for rabbits and other forms of edible wildlife. The risks were great, for to be caught by the bailiffs would mean instant imprisonment or even hanging. The items so got would appear in a mysterious manner on the doorstep of a starving family. The small gang spread their activities over a large area, never using the same source a second time until a good period of time had passed. They had several narrow escapes from capture, danger was never far away. The horrors of this poor, rack-rented district baffle description. The landlords and more often their agents showed no mercy to the poor tenants in small holdings. Inability to pay the rent in most cases meant instant eviction. By the time Francis reached 18 years of age he became the agreed leader of his group of like minded young men. The years spent listening to his grandfather who told him of his experiences as a soldier gave him an insight of how authorities worked, especially the Redcoats and Yeomen (part time soldiers) who supported the landlord class and enforced the laws as required by them. Francis realised that while what little could be done in getting food to the poor, more was needed. He developed into a strong young man, broad shouldered but not overly tall. His long dark hair came down to his shoulders and he grew a beard to match it. In his travels he attended a gathering in the Tyrone town of Castlederg, there he met with a like minded person known as Badger O'Neill. This fearless man was the leader of a similar group of highwaymen; he had been given the name Badger because of his fine head of grey hair and matching beard. This magnificent specimen of manhood could strike terror into anyone who opposed him.

The Badger had heard of the exploits of Proinsias Dubh and invited him to join in some of his exploits. They agreed to meet on a future occasion and make some plans to relieve the wealthy of some of their worldly goods, mainly cash, some of which could be used to pay the rent of the poor. The Badger warned Francis to be very careful when choosing companions to join the group. He said, 'There will always be one who in certain circumstances will betray you either for a reward or through weakness of character'. By now Edward and Moyia were aware of the activities of their son, but realised that some one had to help the poor people. Together they devised a method of disguise for Francis, as Black Francis the Highwayman he would be recognised anywhere. His mother cut off his thick head of black hair and also his beard. With the aid of a portion of sheep skin she made a perfectly fitting wig and false beard. These he wore when going on the exploits and when he and his companions escaped from the scene of a hold up they went their separate ways. Then Francis removed the wig and beard, both along with all the tools of the trade Francis kept in the safety of the crannog, an excellent hiding place. The disguise even deceived his comrades; he never let most of the men see him without them. During the raids the group relieved the rightful owners of money, jewellery, food and anything that could be easily transported. Money in some mysterious manner would find its way to the homes of the poor just in time to pay the rent. Members of the group looked after their own families and close friends, they also bought horses. This enabled them to travel swiftly to areas far from home. Francis kept his own horse on the lands of the Big House where Edward took care of it.

As the accepted leader of the group Frank kept a firm grip on the lads, the proceeds of raids were evenly divided. He had an arrangement with his friend Badger O'Neill whereby all gold coins and some jewellery could be exchanged for silver or copper money. He knew that if a poor tenant paid rent with a gold coin the agent would immediately suspect that it was the proceeds of a robbery. On occasions Francis would join with his friend Badger on his exploits; there was always something new to be learned in the trade. By now members of his own group had armed themselves with pistols, the guns were never used to take life; they were not loaded with shot, only primed with powder and used to scare the victims of a raid. The gang became a source of embarrassment to the land lord class and to the authorities of the land. Rewards were offered for information which could lead to their capture. The group expanded their operations to parts a good distance from their home, travelling by night over rugged territory.

CHAPTER 5

Naturally life became more difficult and the risks were greater, the danger of some person reporting them for a reward increased. Francis had several narrow escapes, on one occasion he sought refuge in a large house, the owner was not aware of his presence. The Red Coats were approaching and a servant girl who was cooking some fish had seen them coming. She could not warn Francis directly as her master would hear her. The girl hit on a plan, as she fried the fish each time she turned it over she said,
"You were never caught for your belly yet". Francis did pick up the repeated message and made good his escape. Another time when he took refuge in a house the Red Coats were ready at the front door not realising that it was one of a very few number of houses with a back door.

At home in Curraghmore life went on pretty much as usual, Edward carried out his duties at the big house and in as far as possible had the confidence of his master Jeffery who still lived above his means and continued to embezzle the estate funds. Francis used the secret hiding place on the Crannog to keep the proceeds of the hold ups and raids on the big houses. The pistols and other weapons were also kept in this safe place and Francis would produce them when required. His wig and false beard were also kept here. Only one or two of his closest friends in the group were aware of the disguise and his real identity. He showed Edward the secret hiding place on the Crannog, for if anything happened to him in was essential that someone should know where the loot was hidden. Most members of the group had either their own horses or access to a steed. The horses were left to graze in the woodlands in an area away from the Red Coats and the bailiffs. The local people knew all about them, but they were not going to tell. The young men always rode the horses without saddles and used rope not leather bridles. All the cash gained from their exploits was carefully divided amongst the members and each had the responsibility of assisting the different families at time of need or when the rent was due.

Francis always kept gold ornaments and jewellery for the others had no way of disposing of them. On occasions when a sentimental piece of jewellery or a ring belonged to a young lady was discovered amongst the 'loot', he found the means to return it to the owner. Rewards were offered for information leading to their capture, they had many narrow escapes and Francis was fully aware that one day their luck would run out. Many false stories were told about the group, they were accused of murder and assaulting people who they held up. This was false, for they were always very careful not to cause hurt or injury to anyone.

It was early in April of 1780 that Francis learned from his network of supporters that on a certain day the mail coach from Donegal to Enniskillen would be carrying some valuable items including gold and silver coin belonging to one of the landlord class. The group for a long time had not carried out any raids in the immediate area. Instead they had travelled further afield to west Fermanagh, south Donegal, Leitrim and Sligo. As the group had not been active in the area for some considerable time the authorities were led into a false sense of security. The coach was due to leave Donegal town early in the morning, it would have a full complement of passengers, six inside and two outside. The coachman was always accompanied by a guard who was armed with a blunderbuss and a brace of pistols. There would be a number of stops along the way to change horses and for the passengers to get refreshments. There was an overnight stop in Irvinestown before proceeding to Enniskillen early the next morning.

Knowing the area well Francis planned the hold up with great care, the lessons that he had learned from his grandfather on military planning would be to his advantage. He chose a place near the Glendurragh River where there was a narrow bridge close to the small village of Kesh. To the west of the bridge was a wooded area where his comrades and the horses could be concealed until the last moment before the coach arrived. One of the men kept watch from a nearby hill top that gave a good view of the road. As a method of stopping the coach Francis got one of the men to lie on the road in a prone position and one of the horses wandering loose nearby. This gave the impression that the rider had been flung from his steed and was badly injured. On arrival at the scene the coachman had no alternative but to rein in the horses and stop, the road of course being to narrow to pass by the injured man. The guard dismounted and with the two male outside passengers went to assist the injured person who was groaning as if in pain. In an instant Francis and his men came out from their hiding places on each side of the road and ordered all hands to surrender and not attempt to use their arms. The people in the coach were not to know that the pistols of the hold up men were not loaded with shot. All the passengers were ordered out of the coach and lined up on the roadside, the coach man was told to secure the reins and apply the brake to the wheels.

Francis ordered the guard to open the large box that contained the money and the mail bags. The man said that he did not have a key as it was kept in the coach office in Enniskillen. Francis took the pistol belonging to the guard and checking that it was loaded and primed, he shot the lock off the box. He removed the bags of coin and some other valuables from the box and choose to ignore the mail. He then turned his attention to the passengers and relieved the men of their purses and watches; he also took pistols from several of the men. He ordered his men not to interfere with the lady passengers some of whom were wearing valuable jewellery. All the loot was placed in a strong bag along with the arms belonging to the guard and the other men. Francis then ordered all hands back on board the coach and told them to proceed on their journey. He and his men then rode their horses into the Glenduraagh River which was quite shallow for a considerable distance; this meant that there were no tracks to show here they had gone. After about a mile they left the river and proceeded overland in a circuitous direction to Curraghmore. At a point in the hills Francis brought the group to a halt, selecting one of them – Sean Reilly – he gave him the bag and its contents and told him to take a different route back to Corraghmore. There he was to give the bag to Edward who would put it in a safe and secure place. As there was always the danger that the group could be ambushed and taken into custody by the Red Coats, Francis also put all the weapons belonging to the group into the bag.

Francis must have had a premonition of what was going to happen for shortly after nightfall the group without any warning was surrounded by about ten Red Coats. The Captain ordered them to dismount and at gun point asked them to account for themselves. Francis said that they were employees of one of the estates and going about their lawful business. The Captain took a closer look and said,
"I know who you are, your name is Black Francis McHugh the highway man, and there is a big reward for your capture". Francis knew the game was up and that at last their luck had run out. As he and his men dismounted and stood by their steeds he spoke to them in Gaelic saying,
"Do now as you would do when we arrive home, give your horse a good clout of you hand on the rump and they will immediately run off" One of the group was a young married man, Peter Ryan, who had a small family. Francis said quietly to Peter,
"In the confusion and darkness jump into that clump of gorse and hide, you may not be discovered". With all the milling around of men and horses and the poor light the Redcoats did not really know how many outlaws they had captured. Peter did as he was told and kept very quiet. The Captain ordered the captives to be tied together with strong ropes, his situation was rather difficult for now the full group could only travel at walking pace. They eventually reached one of the big houses in the area where the prisoners were securely locked up and guards posted around the building. In the morning they were transported by wagons to Enniskillen jail, there to await trial. In the meantime, Peter had left his hiding place and set off for home. As luck would have it after some time he discovered one of the horses grazing peacefully in a field. Mounting it he arrived home at day break and there broke the news that the gang had been captured. Peter and Sean gathered all equipment and evidence of their activities and gave them to Edward who that night brought everything to the crannog. The horses were located and the halters removed from them and also hidden.

CHAPTER 6

Edward, his wife and family now accepted that the reign of Prionsias Dubh had come to an end. There was practically no hope of an escape from Enniskillen Jail. Word came through to the families of the captives that a trial was to take place at a special Assizes to be held in the Month of May 1780. The following is an account of the trial as recorded in the Belfast Newsletter of 6th May 1780.

Extract of a letter from Enniskillen.

This day ended the assizes held here by special commission, at which the following persons were tried and found guilty, upon the clearest evidence; for robbing James Armstrong of Lisgoole, Esq; viz Francis McCue, alias Francis Dough, the captain of the gang, Richard Monkham, Patrick Corrigan, James McCabe, Alex. Wright, and Bryan McAlin. These unhappy, yet daring and dangerous men, having received sentence to be executed. The Judges, Baron Hamilton and Justice Lill, in their charges gave the greatest praise to the Enniskillen Volunteers; and indeed they well deserve the praise and warmest thanks of every man in the county, and particularly of those whose property exposed them to the attacks and ravages of the above desperate gang; and by their watchful attention, in now mounting an officer's guard, they will prevent a possibility of a rescue or escape, until they finish the arduous work they have begun, by seeing the laws of their country fully executed.

The six prisoners were locked up in secure cells in Enniskillen Jail; there they would remain for some days until plans were put in place for the sentence to be carried out. The date for the hanging was set for 12th May 1780. Three men were placed in each cell, Francis and Supple Pat Corrigan and Dick Monan (Monkham) were together, James McCabe, Bryan McAlin and Dan Cleary (known as Alex Wright) in a cell beside them. A gibbet had to be constructed in the jail square and as Francis McHugh would be the first to be hung a coffin had to be made to hold his body. The families, neighbours and friends of the condemned men had assembled outside the building. Included in the group were Edward and Moyia Sweeney and their daughter Sarah Mary. Discussions were going on amongst the judges and officials and it was decided that the hanging of Francis McHugh would ensure that justice was done. The other five prisoners were reprieved, but sentenced to transportation to Australia, a fate that some considered worse than death by hanging. The men knew that there was little or no hope of them escaping from the jail, they talked over many plans but none had any hope of success.

Finally the men thought up a plan whereby one person could be removed from the jail; all agreed that this person should be Prionsias Dubh. Help would be needed from outside and as there was a large group of friends and onlookers around the building it was possible to communicate with them. There at all times was Mary Kane known as Molly, she was a very close friend of Francis and although she never said so was very much in love with him. The young couple were both fluent speakers in the native Gaelic language. This was most important, because in order to put the escape plan into operation certain items were required and a safe method of getting them into the jail had to be worked out. Francis called to Molly in the Gaelic language asking her to come as close as possible and stand under the barred opening of the cell in the wall. He told her to get the members of the crowd to keep some distance away and create as much noise as they could. He would then give instructions to Molly in the Gaelic telling her what he wanted. She was to procure about thirty feet of strong rope, cut into two equal lengths and a similar length of cord. This she could conceal in her clothing and when all was ready she was again to take up a position under the cell opening and get the others to make a lot of noise.

In the cell the men unravelled a woollen garment and with three strands weaved it into a length of wool long enough to reach the ground. It would not be strong enough to haul a rope up into the cell. It would require a weight at the end to carry it to the ground outside. The men tore a piece of material off their clothing and made a pouch; then they removed some of the white washed lime mortar from the cell walls. This was soaked in water to give it more weight, placed into the pouch and secured to the end of the wool line. Francis kept in contact with Molly and gave her further instructions in Gaelic, he told her to have a good supply of poteen available, knowing that the guards would steal it and drink it. The transfer of the strong string and the ropes would have to be made in darkness, preferably in the early hours of the morning when the guards would be less alert.

When Molly had all the required material in her possession and hidden in her clothes; she moved to the wall underneath the window. About a hundred people had assembled as the time for the planned execution was drawing near. The people had burning torches and candles, they were shouting and praying for the prisoners, but remained some distance from the wall. A call from Francis to Molly confirmed that she was in place and ready, the woollen line was dropped and she tied it to the string. Gently Francis hauled it up through the iron bars, next with the help of his comrades they hauled up the strong rope. All the material was hidden under the straw that served as beds for the men. Molly had no idea of what plan was going to be used. With a quick greeting from Francis and one final instruction he told Molly to arrange for his friends Sean Reilly and Peter Ryan to get a wagon to transport his coffin to Curraghmore after the hanging had taken place. Naturally Molly was broken hearted, but Francis consoled her and told her that all would not be as it seemed. Then under cover of the darkness she rejoined the group of people.

Outside work was ongoing building the gallows and making a coffin to hold the body of the condemned man after his execution had taken place. To add insult to injury the authorities would place the coffin into the cell of the person to die on the night before the hanging, which was due to take place after dawn. The plan devised by Francis and his comrades was that with the ropes they would create the 'suicide' of Francis by hanging. One section of rope would be used to support the weight of his body by being placed under his arms looped around one of the bars in the opening up the wall of the cell. The free end was then secured around the loop under his arms using a special knot that was very easy to undo. This took the full weight of his body. The other piece of rope was made into a noose and placed around his neck and also secured to one of the bars. The woollen cord and the strong string were concealed around Francis's waist.

The men practiced this method several times to ensure that the tension of both ropes was fully correct, and everything went according to plan. The fake hanging was to take place in the hours of darkness before the dawn. The guards brought the coffin into the cell during the night and placed it against the wall, telling Francis that the next day he would be in it. The carpenters had done a crude bit of work with rough wood and there were gaps where the boards joined together. About three o'clock in the morning everything was prepared, using water, Dick Corrigan made a paste from the white wash plaster on the cell walls; this he rubbed into Francis's face to give him a ghostly appearance. Using the coffin as a base for Francis to stand on, the ropes were put into place and Francis suspended from the bars. Dick and Pat tumbled the coffin away from Francis's feet and his friend was safely suspended. Dick, Pat and their comrades in the next cell then raised the alarm, shouting and rattling the bars of the cell door to get the attention of the guards who soon arrived on the scene, some were only half awake and others were suffering from the effects of the poteen that they had stolen and drank. Dick said that he had been waken by a noise and discovered Francis's dead body hanging from the bars. The guards unlocked the cell door and by the light of torches saw for them selves the gruesome sight of the 'dead' outlaw hanging at the end of the rope. There was uproar amongst the guards and the Captain came on the scene.

He ordered the 'body' to be taken down; Dick Monan and Pat Corrigan rushed to help. While the guards removed from the bar, the rope that was around the victim's neck, Dick and Pat supported the body and when the weight was off, slipped the knot off the hidden rope and tucked it into the back of Francis's garments. The body was then placed on the cell floor. Dick shouted and roared that some of the guards must have come into the cell when he and Pat were asleep, over powered Francis and hung him from the bars. The Captain was in a quandary and could see a certain amount of truth in the claim made by Dick. The three other comrades joined in the uproar and argument, saying that there was no other way that Francis could have hung himself and that they would swear the guards carried out this dastardly act. After some discussion with a few of his more sober comrades, the Captain decided that the best story to tell was that somehow a length of rope had been smuggled into the jail and with it Francis McHugh had committed suicide. The body was placed into the coffin and the carpenter brought in to nail the lid on. The fact that the boards were not a good fit and had space between them meant that Francis would have a supply of air. The Captain consulted with his superiors and one of the Judges, they came to the decision that as the prisoner was now dead and had cheated the hangman out of his fee, justice had been done and that his body should be handed over to his family for burial as was the normal procedure after an execution.

CHAPTER 7

As instructed by Molly, Sean and Peter had obtained a horse and wagon, which they put into a yard just outside Enniskillen town. Four strong soldiers carried the coffin out of the Jail and handed it over to friends of Francis McHugh. It was carried in relays to the town boundary followed by many of the people who had held the vigil at the jail. A number of Yeomen accompanied the cortege as far as the boundary and then retuned to Enniskillen. When it was safe to do so Sean and Peter took the wagon out to the road and the coffin was placed on it. A heart broken Molly was asked by the two men to join them aboard the wagon while the rest followed on foot. As they travelled along the young folk discussed the events of the day, a variety of suggestions were made as to the outcome of the death of Francis. Even in her sorrow Molly said that everything was so unusual that it was difficult for her to understand. She told the two men how Francis had got her to find the rope and how in a fool proof manner it was smuggled into the jail. All agreed that Francis was not the type of person to take his own life no matter what were the circumstances. One suggestion was that Francis and one of his comrades had exchanged their clothing and identities and his friend was then hung in the cell. This would mean that Francis would then be transported to Australia.

After about an hours travel from Enniskillen the wagon was a considerable distance ahead of the group who were on foot. The young people stopped at a roadside well to have a drink and to give the horse a drink and a rest. Sean thought that he heard a noise coming from inside the coffin; he drew the attention of the others to this. Listening carefully they heard a tapping sound and then a muffled voice saying.
"Do not be alarmed – it is I – Francis and I am very much alive". There with the aid of a branch of a tree found on the roadside Peter removed the boards that comprised the lid of the coffin. Inside they found Francis very much alive and well, but a bit stiff and sore not having been fit to move for a long time. There was great joy to discover that he was alive and well. They assisted him from his hiding place and refreshed him with a drink of water. They decided to resume their journey as they did not at this stage want the walking group know about the secret. Francis told his friends how the fake hanging had been staged and he thanked Molly for making it possible. Only his very closest friends were aware of the disguise used by Francis, now he removed his wig and false beard. Molly, Sean and Peter were amazed at the difference this made in his appearance. He also removed his cloak which had been specially made by his mother. Turning it inside out the cloak was a different colour and design. Naturally there was great jubilation amongst the four friends, but they still had to be most careful to ensure that only the most trusted of friends would learn of the great escape.

Some distance along the road the travellers came to a cabin and outside it there was a poor woman and three young children, she was obviously in a state of great distress. Stopping the wagon Molly went to help the woman, who told her that her husband had died with the fever and she did not know what to do. She had no means to give her man a proper burial and nobody to help her. Francis told Sean and Peter to conceal the wagon in some trees near the cabin and they then went inside to see the situation for themselves. They told the woman that they had a coffin in the wagon and that they would use it to bury her husband. In a short time they had placed the body in the coffin, nailed on the lid again and placed it in the wagon. They set off once again on their journey; the group of walking mourners could be seen approaching in the distance. All being well they should reach the old cemetery at Carn just about night fall. There a grave had been dug to hold what the people and the authorities thought would be the mortal remains of Black Francis McHugh - Highway Man. Francis, Sean and Peter walked beside the wagon while Molly, the children and their grieving mother sat on it. In the graveyard all the friends and neighbours had assembled for the funeral, very few were aware of the real identity of Black Francis. Soon they were joined by the mourners who had walked from Enniskillen jail.

Molly had run back to meet them and to quietly tell Moyia, Edward and Mary Sarah what the real situation was and let them know that Francis was very much alive. She warned them to still act the part of a heart broken family as there would be spies present who would report everything that happened to the authorities. After the funeral the Sweeney family took care of the young woman and her children, they found them a place to live and gave them money to buy food and the other necessities of life.

CHAPTER 8

Francis was smart enough to realise that his short career as a highway man had now come to a close, he remembered the old Irish proverb "Long runs the fox but in the end he gets caught". Several matters needed his attention; from the proceeds of the raids carried out he divided money amongst the families of his comrades. The relations of the men who were transported to Australia were taken care of - for the foreseeable future they would not be evicted for non payment of the rent of their holdings. He made a generous contribution to the widow of the man who was buried in his name in Carn graveyard. All that remained now was a considerable amount of valuable jewellery hidden along with weapons and other items on the crannog in Curraghmore. Francis had a plan for the hidden treasures. He had learned from Edward all about the activities of Jeffery Badham and how he had de-frauded his master, Sir Albert Melgard, by falsifying the accounts. He knew the layout of the big house and where Jeffery kept his ill-gotten gains. Francis was determined to make Jeffery pay for the many crimes against the tenants and the young girls whose lives he had destroyed. He and Molly had become firm friends, they hoped to marry and then immigrate to Australia where they would join the other family members who were now well settled there. Francis could possibly do something to help his former comrades who had been transported.

Francis and Edward discussed the serious situation created by the fraudulent behaviour of Jeffery Badham. By his embezzlement and criminal management of the accounts of the estate of Sir Albert Melgard he was really putting extreme pressure on the poor tenants of the area. The men were convinced, that if Sir Albert could be made aware of the situation there could be a considerable reduction in the rents. Careful planning was needed, Edward had the knowledge of Jeffery's movements and how he would on occasions travel by coach to Dublin to meet some of his lady friends. These trips usually lasted for almost a week. Edward knew of the secret hiding place for the key to the cabinet in Jeffery's office, he had also at one time found a spare key for the lock on the study door. Francis struck on a plan that should meet their requirements; first he needed a sheet of the official letter paper and one of the embossed envelopes from the study in the house. Early in July Jeffery Badham left for Dublin on the mail coach, on a rare visit to the house by Francis, the office door was left unlocked by arrangement with Edward. Francis entered the room and closing the door made a visual inspection of the study; he also unlocked the cabinet and made himself familiar with its contents. Leaving everything as he found it and ensuring that he had not been observed he left the house. He had taken with him the stationery he required to put his plan into operation. Bringing with him a quill and ink Francis went out to the secret place on the Crannog, there he compiled the following letter.

County Fermanagh.

9th July 1780.

To:- Sir Albert Melgard.
Landlord.
Castle Leslough.

Sir,
On behalf of the tenants of this part of your estate I feel that it is my duty to make you aware of the conduct of your agent - Jeffery Bedham, Esq. For many years your trusted agent has been embezzling the funds from the estate, he has retained a percentage of the rents collected for his own purposes using them to fund an immoral life with a selection of mistresses and leading a high life considerably above his means. In a most fraudulent way he has kept two sets of records, one showing the true income from your estate and the other set of records he presents to you for inspection on your visits to his house.

As Mr. Jeffery is at present on a trip to Dublin and will remain there for at least one week, I suggest that you be in attendance in his house upon his return. His office is always kept locked, but on your arrival a key will be in the lock. In the office is a secure cabinet, you are to reach up to the top of the office door, there in a recess you will find a key to the cabinet. Inside there is the evidence you require and a considerable amount of his ill gotten gains. You will understand that I cannot disclose my name, but should you consider the information I have given you of some value and worthy of reward, I suggest that you give your tenants in the area a considerable reduction in rent and a guarantee of their tenancy in their holdings.

I remain your obedient but anonymous servant.

That evening Francis made his preparations to travel the long journey to the home of Sir Albert Melgard, a distance of over 50 miles. He packed some food and water into a knapsack and placed the sealed envelope in the pocket of his cloak. From his knowledge of the countryside he chose a route that for the most part he could travel unobserved. Should he by chance be stopped by a patrol of soldiers he would show them the letter for Sir Albert telling them that it was an important message from his agent Jeffery Badham. Having travelled through the night Francis came within sight of Castle Leslough. Hiding his steed in a clump of bushes he proceeded up the avenue and made his way to the entrance used by tradesmen and messengers. His knock on the door was answered by a servant, Francis handed him the letter telling him that it was very important that it be given to his Lordship immediately. He then left and returned to his horse unobserved and set off for home.

After a rest and a meal Francis went to Ardnamona House and had a conversation with Edward, he told him that he had a plan to expose Badham, it was better that Edward should not know any details of the plan as he could possibly be questioned about a coming event. As part of the plan it was necessary for Francis to make another visit to the Jeffery Badham's study. The best time to do this was late in the evening when the servants had all their duties carried out. Francis then went out to the Crannog where the proceeds of the hold-ups were cached. Practically all the money had been distributed to the families of his comrades who been transported and to other families who were in need. There remained a considerable amount of jewellery and other valuables that it had not been possible to dispose of. Francis placed all the items into a mail pouch that had come from the hold-up of a mail coach. All the weapons used by the gang which would no longer be needed, he placed in a sack. He brought all with him to the big house and getting a signal from Edward that the coast was clear he made his way to the office. Opening the locked cabinet he removed a leather pouch from a drawer, the pouch contained a large amount of gold and silver coins, the proceeds of the income from rent and livestock sales that Jeffery had taken for his own use. Francis placed the mail pouch with all the jewellery in it in the drawer where the money had been, he then put the sack full of weapons inside the cabinet, which he locked and returned the key to it hiding place. He secured the office door and quietly left the house, passing by the workshop he gave Edward a signal that all was well.

Back in the castle Sir Albert was outraged when he opened and read the letter when it was handed to him by the butler. The contents indicated to him that the criminal fraud, swindling and deception by his agent were on a greater scale than that which he had suspected for some time. Any landlord accepted that his agents would cream off a certain amount of the income of the part of the estate they managed. He ordered the butler to prepare his coach for a journey to Curraghmore. He called on the Captain of his Yeomen to select his ten best horsemen to accompany him on the journey. The party arrived at Ardnamona House shortly after Jeffery Badham had returned from Dublin. He was puzzled and surprised to see Sir Albert arriving, as he was not due for some time to make one of his regular inspections. The Landlord directed his agent to lead him to the office, Jeffery knew by the attitude of his boss that some serious situation had cropped up. When ordered to open the cabinet, Jeffery flustered and blustered, saying that he had mislaid the key. Sir Albert immediately reached up to the top of the door and took down the key which he handed to Badham and ordered him to open the cabinet. There he spotted the bag containing the guns and other weapons that had belonged to outlaw gang. Opening the drawer and seeing the mail pouch he took this out and emptied the contents on the desk, he was amazed to see the large collection of valuable jewellery.

"You wicked scoundrel; this evidence tells me that you have been involved with the Black Francis McHugh gang of highway men who have terrorised this area for several years". Next he turned his attention to the record books containing the accounts for the estate. Sir Albert then called in the Captain of his guard and instructed him to arrest Badham and escort him to Enniskillen jail. Sir Albert then assembled all the servants and farm staff in the courtyard where he informed them that Jeffery Badham had been dismissed from his post and that soon he would be appointing a new agent. The landlord planned to stay in the house until everything was organised. When Edward returned home that night he told Moyia, Francis and Sarah Mary the story of the undignified end to the reign of Jeffery Badham. They later learned that he gone completely mad and was committed to an asylum for the mentally insane, there he would end his days in disgrace. Sir Albert decided that there would be no point in bringing his agent before the legal courts. He recognised some of the jewellery as belonging to friends of his, a few discreet inquiries found the owners of most of the remainder and he had it returned to them. He also informed the tenants that their rents would be considerably reduced and gave them a guarantee to remain on their holdings.

CHAPTER 9

Francis took the hoard of gold coins and hid them on the Crannog; next he made contact with his friend, Badger O'Neill and arranged to have a considerable portion of the gold coins converted into silver which he could distribute to the families of Richard Monan, Patrick Corrigan, James McCabe, Dan Cleary and Bryan McAlin. He gave Badger a good deal on the exchange and told him of his plans to immigrate to Australia and informed him that he could now take over his territory and look after the poor should they be victimised by unjust land lords and their agents. Francis kept aside a sufficient portion of the gold to pay for the passage of Molly and himself to Australia and to buy property in that country. There he would contact his uncle Jack McHugh and hopefully buy a sizeable portion of land and found a farm.

Meanwhile back in Ardnamona House - Sir Albert Melgard decided to remain in residence for several months during 1781 and have this part of his estate re-organised. He decided to appoint one of his nephews, George Melgard as his agent. The present members of staff were to be retained including Edward Sweeney, on visits to the farmyard and stables Sir Albert had seen how Edward kept the place in an orderly way, all machinery was in perfect working order, horses and other livestock well cared for. He complimented Edward on all of this and also sought his advice on matters concerning the estate. Sir Albert instructed Edward to contact as many of the tenants as possible and inform them that the exorbitant rents fixed by his former agent – Jeffery Badham – where to be reduced considerably and the tenancy of their holdings would be guaranteed in all reasonable circumstances. For a considerable time Elisabeth Badham and her daughter – Jennifer – had spent most of her time with her aunt who lived in a large house near Enniskillen. Sir Albert now arranged for all her furniture and personal belonging to be delivered to Elisabeth by wagon. He also granted her a suitable annual pension that would enable her to live in reasonable comfort.

Francis had received word that a travelling Friar would soon be in the area so he and Molly made their way to a remote Mass rock where the Friar would celebrate a Mass, baptise children, officiate at marriages and give the sacraments to those requiring them. In the presence of their parents and other family members Francis and Molly became man and wife. Now they were in a position to plan their passage to Australia where they would join Uncle Jack McHugh. By this time George Melgard had taken up his position in Ardnamona House as the agent for his uncle. Before departing for Castle Leslough, Sir Albert spoke to Edward and told him how much he appreciated all that he was doing on the estate. He also said that if he could do anything at all reasonable for Edward or his family he had only to ask. Edward took the opportunity to make one request saying,

"My son, Francis Sweeney who has recently been married intends to immigrate to Australia with his wife – Molly. If you would be kind enough to give him a reference which would enable him to find employment and possibly acquire some property I would be forever grateful to you". Sir Albert said, "I will be very pleased to do as you request, in fact I am part owner of a vessel that trades between England and Australia. I will also give you a letter of introduction to the Captain Eric Vernon and your son and his wife will have a government assisted passage at a reduced rate. The ship 'Minerva' departs from Liverpool in July 1783 and calls in Dublin within a month, weather being favourable. Your son and his wife can join the ship in Dublin". Sir Albert then added that an acquaintance of his, Sir Henry Davidson was Lieutenant General of New South Wales. Edward was to present his letter of reference to Sir Henry when the ship arrived in Sydney and he would be assisted in finding a position in the country.

Francis and Molly organised their plans for the long voyage to Australia. Edward constructed a fine large cabin trunk for the young couple; it was made of oak with the corners bound in strong leather. He fitted the lid with heavy brass hinges and a strong lock to keep the contents secure. Moyia who had inherited the many skills and crafts from her mother including that of dress making got a big roll of home spun tweed. From this she designed and made a long dress for Molly. It was very important that the gold coins which the couple were taking to Australia should be well hidden in a most secure place. There was always the danger of thieves stealing any valuables from travellers. Moyia covered some coins in the material that the dress was made from and sewed them on as buttons. She then made a special double lined belt and at intervals secured a number of coins in it. In the trunk Edward built in some secret compartments to hold more of the gold coins and other valuables. Francis was hopeful that in Australia he could find his comrades, Pat Corrigan, Dick Monan, James McCabe, Bryan McAlin and Dan Cleary and give them help to get free from their sentence.

Francis and Molly were given a cabin of their own on 'The Minerva'. Molly like most of her age group did not have any schooling or education; she was a most intelligent young woman. Before leaving Dublin, Francis purchased a journal to record the story of the voyage. Using this book, Francis on the voyage, taught Molly how to read and write. Not only did she record details of the voyage but she also wrote the full story of life in Curraghmore, the experience of Moyia, the birth of Francis and his career as a highwayman. After an uneventful but long voyage Francis and Molly arrived in Sydney early in 1784.

Over the years letters home to the family in Curraghmore related how the couple settled down in Australia. Assisted by Uncle Jack McHugh and using the letters of recommendation from Sir Albert Melgard Francis found a good job and eventually bought his own large sheep farm. He and Molly had a family of two boys and two girls, but never again were they to return to Ireland.

THE IRISH HIGHWAY MAN

An Irish Highway Man had few if any equals in the profession, generally a perfectionist in his trade. The scourge of the landlord class, the Mail Coaches and authority in general. The saviour of the down trodden poor who lived in poverty, a miserable often brutal existence, principally because of Rack Rents imposed on tenants by ruthless landlords.

Many of them had served in the armies of continental countries and so received the finest military training. The Highway Man had the many skills necessary to pursue his chosen trade, as a horseman, marksman, swordsman and a strategic mind he had few equals. To the authorities he was a criminal, an outlaw, a scoundrel, a rebel, a scourge to the country who fully deserved to end his life on the gibbet swinging from the end of a rope. He shared the proceeds of his trade with the poor who considered him a swashbuckling outlaw and adventurer who risked his life to help poor people facing eviction by tyrannical landlords. While he was often given shelter in the cabins of the poor he also had to contend with the risk of being betrayed by an informer for a miserable reward.

He was a dangerous figure on the tracks and roads, considered to be a dashing romantic thief, a rebel who risked his life to help the less fortunate. His command "Stand and Deliver" as he brandished a brace of pistols, was reputed to have originated in the House of Parliament. When a vital vote was to be taken, the Speaker is said to have told the members, "This is the time to stand and deliver". Meaning that the members must courageously stand up and be counted to deliver their votes.

In the era of the Highway man the dreaded words, "Stand and Deliver" was a command to the driver of the coach to halt, who clearly understood that he was going to be relieved of all valuable cargo and his passengers had to hand over their purses and jewellery.

Men like Black Francis McHugh plied their trade in the later half of the eighteenth century and the early part of the nineteenth century. Their exploits remain in Irish folklore and have lost nothing in the telling.

Dedication

This is for me book number seven, not many years ago I would never have foreseen that I might some day become an author. It is but right that this book should be dedicated to a number of people who have helped me over the years. First must be my wife Ina who has always supported this hobby of mine, then our sons and daughters, my brothers and sisters who have always had an interest in the books I had published. I can say that I served a rather amateurish apprenticeship to journalism under the guidance of Willie John Duffy, editor of the Belleek page in the Fermanagh news. Willie would often ask me to contribute a report on matters of local interest. He would correct my many errors and add his own sense of humour to what otherwise would be a basic story.

Book number one, the first real attempt to produce a proper book was, when in 1992 Ann Monaghan, Charlie Ward and myself compiled, "The Church Upon the Hill" to mark the centenary of St. Patrick's Church, Belleek. Two good friends who contributed to this book are sadly no longer with us, Sister Elizabeth Smith wrote a moving letter of how she grew up in the parish. Fr. Seamus McManus then Parish Priest of Aghaloo, Aughnacloy wrote the Preface. The art work of our daughter Jane illustrated incidents of the pre camera age in a way that contributed immensely to the enjoyment of the readers.

Book number two a history of the "West Fermanagh Kingdoms of Mulleek and Toura" was produced in 1998 under the guidance of noted Irvinestown historian, author and highly valued friend, Breege McCusker who also kindly wrote the foreword. The graphic design and layout was done expertly by James McGrath then on the staff of the Donegal Democrat. The Preface was written by another family friend of long standing, Rev. Nigel D.J. Kirkpatrick, B.Th. of St. Columba's Church, Portadown. Once again the art work of daughter Jane has by her illustrations added in no small way to the production of this book.

Book number three, was in 2003 the first venture into the realm of fiction. "The Phantom Airman" is a mixture of fiction and historical fact covering 1500 years. This story owes its existence to journalist - Gerry McLaughlin – who in the Irish News, Sept.

19th 1992 wrote an article containing memories of World War 11 in the Belleek district. He suggested that an airman based in one of the radio stations in Belleek had imbibed more well that wise in a rural Shebeen had lost his way while crossing the bog on a foggy night and was never seen again. Gerry wrote that there was the making of a great story slumbering somewhere in Fermanagh on this mythical person. Being then busy working on 'The Church Upon the Hill' I preserved the article in place where things to be done are stored. I felt that the story was so good that it would need the talents of a professional writer. I suggest this to a number of such people who for one reason or another did not consider it suitable. The best advice I got was when I discussed it with Mary Pat Kelly, New York T.V. producer and journalist who said to me, "Joe if you want that book written, just do it your self". Having prepared the manuscript I invited a number of well qualified friends to read it and proof read it and give me their opinion on the merits of the story. Breege McCusker was most enthusiastic, Susan Catherine Schneider, author of Oregon, U.S.A., Maire Carr, a legal secretary, London, my sister Eileen Aiken, retired teacher, Ardee, Co. Louth, Anne Palmer, journalist, Enniskillen, her aunt Kathleen Palmer, Librarian, Enniskillen, my nephew, Brian O'Loughlin, newspaper editor, Jutta Tyler, Author, Kinlough, Co. Leitrim. Patricia Brooks, author and retired school teacher of New Zealand whose ancestors came from Belleek. Having read and corrected my many mistakes all of the above keep the pressure on me to have "The Phantom Airman" published. Soon the manuscript was presented to James McGrath and his worthy assistant, my cousin Sinéad Fox. James was by now managing Diamond Sign Printing, again he did an excellent design on this book.

Book number four "Voices of the Donegal Corridor" contains many stories of the planes that crashed in Fermanagh and Donegal during World War 11 was published by Nonsuch, Dublin in 2005. Once again Breege McCusker made a major contribution to this book as did the families of airmen from various parts of the world. They supplied me with very valuable information and useful photographs. For the many ceremonies we held to unveil memorial stones in memory of the young airmen who died in crashes we received invaluable help from Commandant Sean Curran of the 28th Infantry Battalion, Finner Camp, Ballyshannon. This book was launched for me in the Fermanagh County Library, Enniskillen by Edward O'Loghlen of the Medical Library, Galway University. Edward was the organiser of the 2005 O'Loughlin Clan Reunion in The Burren, Co. Clare.

Book number five "Old Belleek Town" also published by Nonsuch in 2006. For this I received many previously unpublished photographs from a number of local people who wish to remain nameless. It has also been enhanced by the art work of Jane O'Loughlin. It brought great pleasure to the many exiles from the area now living in far off countries.

Book number six "A History of Camlin Castle and the Tredennick Family". Here I revert once again to self publishing and avail of the expertise of James McGrath and Diamond Sign Printing. The finished product is proof of this decision. My thanks once again to Breege McCusker for her support and fitting Foreword. I was fortunate that Camlin Castle was perhaps the only major building and family estate in the area that had not already been historically documented. The arrival in Belleek in September 2006 of Wendy Tredennick/Henderson and her cousin Mary Tredennick who sought my help in tracing the family connection to the area provided me with the incentive and invaluable information to proceed with this work. Wendy kindly wrote a most suitable Preface for the book. At a later stage their cousin Jenny who lives in Magherafelt joined the team.

The tragic death of local journalist Donna Marie Ferguson in whose memory the book is dedicated is suitably coupled with the history of Camlin Castle. In the planning and design of the book I was ably guided and advised by another good friend – Eileen Hewson – a highly talented author in a different field.

Book number seven is a return to the realm of fiction. A rumour circulated in this area during World War 11 that a German plane had crashed into the moor lands and disappeared without trace led me to write a story 'Lost in Ireland'. Once again I have been advised and guided by Eileen Hewson and of course my usual adviser – Breege McCusker. With so many faithful advisors and friends it is not a wonder that my publications have been successful considering my status as an amateur who lacks any academic qualifications. To all these wonderful people I dedicate this work.